this book belongs to

McKenzie.................

Thank you, kittie - love Rose x

Billy x

Goats

Gruff x

Prince Florian

Little Miss M

Swan Princess

For K&E, and for Luke and Jack Gibson - A.L.

For Kathryn - L.B.

THE FAIRYTALE HAIRDRESSER AND SNOW WHITE
A PICTURE CORGI BOOK 978 0 552 56777 0
Published in Great Britain by Picture Corgi, an imprint of Random House
Children's Publishers UK. A Penguin Random House Company

Penguin
Random House
UK

This edition published 2014

5 7 9 10 8 6

www.randomhousechildrens.co.uk
www.randomhouse.co.uk

Addresses for companies within The Random House Group Limited
can be found at: www.randomhouse.co.uk/offices.htm
THE RANDOM HOUSE GROUP Limited Reg. No. 954009
A CIP catalogue record for this book is available from the British Library.
Printed in China

MIX
Paper from
responsible sources
FSC® C018179
FSC
www.fsc.org

Penguin Random House is committed to a
sustainable future for our business, our readers
and our planet. This book is made from Forest
Stewardship Council® certified paper.

The Fairytale Hairdresser

and

SNOW WHITE

Abie Longstaff
&
Lauren Beard

PICTURE CORGI

Kittie Lacey was the best hairdresser in all the land.

Customers came from far, far away to have their hair styled,
their tails plaited and their beards trimmed.

Kittie's salon was the perfect place to hang out.
Cinderella baked biscuits for everyone,
Rapunzel loved hearing about the latest
hairstyles, and Rose, the Sleeping Beauty,
always made full use of the comfy sofa.

One day Kittie and her friends were flicking through their favourite magazine, *The Looking Glass*.

"Look at this!" said Rapunzel, pointing to an article about a princess called Snow White.

SNOW WHITE MISSING:
WHO'S TO BLAME?

PRINCESS SNOW WHITE HAS VANISHED FROM THE PALACE!
In a statement to the press, the magic mirror from the palace said:

"I am the mirror on the wall,
I said Snow White was fairest of all.
The Queen was angry. I heard her say,
'Take that Snow White far away.'

She made the huntsman bring his knife.
So Snow White ran to save her life."

NONSENSE!
When we put Mr Mirror's words to the Queen, she claimed they were utter nonsense. "I wouldn't hurt anyone," she said, "not even Snow White, with her shiny black hair, her ruby-red lips, and her skin as white as snow. I'm far too beautiful to be mean."

SECOND DISAPPEARANCE
In a recent shocking twist, Mr Mirror has now also disappeared from the palace.

In an exclusive interview with *The Looking Glass*, the huntsman stated: "It's all the Queen's fault. She tried to make me hurt Snow White but I couldn't do it. I told Snow White to run as far from the Queen as she could."

The Queen was not available for further comment as she was busy having her eyebrows shaped into an evil arch.

"Oh no!" said Kittie.

"Poor Snow White," said Cinderella.

"I hope she's ok," said Rapunzel.

"Yes," said Rose. "That Queen sounds nasty."

Later that day, Red Riding Hood came to see Kittie. "Hiya," she said. "I found this mirror on my way home from Grandma's house. I thought you might like it for the salon."
"Oh, thank you," said Kittie.

Moon beam Shampoo

STAR DUST SPRAY

Kitten fur tamer

To kittie love Rose & Florian x

The mirror had a blue glow and seemed to shimmer strangely in the light.

Ding Dong! Just then the door opened and in came seven dwarves for seven haircuts and seven beard-trims.

"Can you keep a secret?" said the eldest dwarf, as Kittie chopped and trimmed. "We're hiding a runaway!"

"Yes," said the youngest. "She's so kind."

"She has shiny black hair."

"And ruby-red lips."

"Her skin is as white as snow."

"She's always singing, just like me."

"And she loves apples."

Suddenly the mirror shimmered and shook and, to Kittie's amazement, a face appeared. The dwarves gasped as the mirror began to speak.

"I know that girl, she's called Snow White. Tell me, tell me, am I right?"

"Yes!" said the youngest dwarf. "That's her."

"The Queen's on her way with an evil plot.
I'd tell you more, but that's all I've got."

The mirror shimmered again and the face disappeared.

"Quick!" said the eldest dwarf. "Come on, everyone."

They rushed to the dwarves'
house as quickly as they could . . .

and there in the kitchen stood a girl. She had shiny black hair,
ruby-red lips and skin as white as snow. She sang a little song
as she made an apple pie.

It was Snow White!

"It's lucky the dwarves have hidden you away," said Kittie.
"The Wicked Queen is coming!"
"Oh no!" said Snow White. "What shall I do?"
"Don't worry," said Kittie, "I'll help you. Come to my salon
and I'll fix it so that the Queen won't recognize you."

Back at the salon,
Kittie gave Snow
White all kinds of
disguises to try on.
It took quite a while . . .

but finally they found the perfect disguise.

"No one will recognize you now," said Kittie,
as she brushed Snow White's new hair.
"We'll pretend you're my assistant."

"Thank you!" said Snow White.
"But, oh . . ." she sighed sadly.
"What's wrong?" asked Kittie.
"Well, there is someone I **do** want
to recognize me. He works on the
high street – he's lovely. I think he
likes me, but now he won't know
who I am."

Kittie gave Snow White a hug. "We'll find a way to get that Wicked Queen locked up for good," she promised. "Then I'll make you look like yourself again – you'll be the fairest of them all."

The very next day an old pedlar woman came
to town with a basket of juicy red apples.

She tapped at the door of the bike shop.
"Have you seen a girl with shiny black hair?"
she asked.
"No," said Red.

She tapped at the door of the optician.
"Have you seen a girl with ruby-red lips?"
she asked. "Her skin is as white as snow."
"No," growled Mr Wolf.

The old woman tapped on the door of Kittie's salon.
A girl came to the door. Her hair was purple,
her lips were pink . . .
but her skin was as white as snow.
"Hmmm," said the old woman.

The girl was singing a little song.
"Ah," said the old woman.

"Oh, apples!" the girl cried. "My favourite!"
"Aha!" said the old woman, and she gave the girl a juicy red apple.
The girl took a big bite and . . .

. . . fell to the floor.
"Snow White!"
cried Kittie,
hurrying to
her side.

"Now I am the fairest of them all," cackled the old woman as she hurried away. But as she ran her disguise slipped off. It was the wicked queen!

Snow White lay as still as stone on the salon floor.
Kittie didn't know what to do . . .

Suddenly Kittie remembered the magic mirror.
"Mirror, mirror on the wall,
Who's the best doctor of them all?"
The mirror shimmered and shook.

"I know a prince who's
a doctor too –
High Street, number 42.
Dr Charming is the best,
he'll wake poor Snow White
from her rest."

Kittie opened her salon door.
"Mr Gingerbread Man!" she cried.
"Please hurry and fetch Dr Charming.
Run, run, as fast as you can!"
So Mr Gingerbread Man ran.

Before long he came running back,
and with him was Dr Charming.

"Snow White!" cried Dr Charming, and he bent down
to pick up the beautiful princess.

But as he lifted her, the piece of apple shifted in her throat . . .
Snow White coughed and slowly opened her eyes.
"Thank goodness," said Kittie.

"Hello, Snow White," said Dr Charming, as he held her in his arms.
Snow White smiled. "How did you know it was me?"

"I'd recognize you anywhere," said Dr Charming.

As soon as he heard what had happened, the
Grand Old Duke set out to capture the Wicked
Queen. He marched his men to the top of the
hill and he marched them down again.

The Queen was marched off to prison,
and Snow White was safe at last!

Many weeks later, Snow White and Dr Charming were married. There was a huge party, and Fairyland's favourite band played all their most popular hits.

DOUG
& THE
DELVERS

And, of course, Kittie Lacey
was on hand to make sure
Snow White was the
fairest of them all.